BY THE SAME AUTHOR

DICK KING-SMITH

Three Terrible Trins

ILLUSTRATED BY MARK TEAGUE

SCHOLASTIC INC.

New York Toronto London Auckland Sydney
Mexico City New Delhi Hong Kong

ISBN 0-590-96808-4

Text copyright © 1994 by Fox Busters, Ltd.
Illustrations copyright © 1994 by Mark Teague.
All rights reserved. Published by Scholastic Inc., 555 Broadway, New York, NY 10012, by arrangement with Crown Publishers, Inc.

SCHOLASTIC and associated logos are trademarks and/or registered trademarks of Scholastic Inc.

12 11 10 9 8   6 7 8/0

Printed in the U.S.A.

CONTENTS

1 THREE BOYS

At six o'clock on the morning of her birthday, Mrs. Gray's husband was killed and eaten.

It was her first birthday, and he was her third husband.

Both of her previous mates had died violent deaths, and now Mr. Gray, who was a trifle near-sighted, had not seen the cat coming.

"I really know how to pick 'em," said Mrs. Gray to a friend who had brought the sad news. "First Brown goes and steps on a mousetrap, then Black falls into the tropical fish tank, and now Gray's gone, and on my birthday, of all days."

"Many happy returns, dear," said the friend.

Mrs. Gray sniffed loudly.

"I shall never marry again," she said. "Never. I shall devote my life to my fatherless children."

Mrs. Gray had in fact given birth to twenty

1

children in all. By the late Mr. Brown she had had seven cubs, by the late Mr. Black ten more, and these had all left home to make their way in the world, many now with children of their own.

The recently deceased Mr. Gray's cubs were, rather disappointingly, just three in number, and only a few days old.

Mrs. Gray looked sadly at them as they squirmed in the nest, pink and blind and hairless.

"Poor little trins," she murmured.

"Pardon?" said the friend.

"Trins," said Mrs. Gray, "is another word for triplets. My old granny told me that. It's supposed to be an unlucky number, she always said. She taught me a rhyme about it.

'How sad the mother mouse must be
 Whose litter numbers only three.
 The gravest of all mousely sins
 Is to produce a set of trins.' "

"Try not to worry, dear," said the friend. "They're fine-looking cubs. By the way, what are they?"

"Three bucks," said Mrs. Gray.

"All boys, eh?" said the friend. "They'll soon be up to mischief."

"So long as they aren't as careless as Brown or as clumsy as Black or as blind as my latest late husband," said Mrs. Gray.

"What are you going to call them?"

"Oh, I don't know. Tom, Dick, and Harry—what does it matter?"

"Rather common names, dear, don't you think?" said the friend.

"All right, then, I'll call them Thomas, Richard, and Henry," said the widow. "That's a bit posher."

And this is the story of Thomas, Richard, and Henry Gray—the terrible trins.

2 FOUR FLOORS

The farmhouse in which Mrs. Gray lived—along with dozens and dozens of other mice—was large and old and rambling. Below it was a cellar, and above it was an attic, and over several hundreds of years countless generations of mice had lived (and died) within its walls and beneath its floorboards.

These small inhabitants of Orchard Farm were broadly divided into four tribes, or clans, according to which level they occupied.

The clan that lived at the very top of the house took their name from their surroundings, and they were simply called the Attics.

On the floor below them dwelled the Ups (short for Upstairs Mice), and under them, on the ground floor, were the Downs.

At the bottom of the pile lived the Cellarmice.

All the clans were able to visit one another, sometimes to interbreed, sometimes to fight, by using a network of mouse-made channels and tunnels and stairways that threaded up and down through the old farmhouse.

The Attics thought themselves superior both to the comfort-loving Ups and to the greedy Downs, who lived as close as possible to the rooms where food was to be found—the kitchen, the pantry, and the dining room.

Both Ups and Attics needed to descend nightly, and sometimes daily, to scavenge, but for the Attics the journey was longer and more hazardous. Accordingly, they were a lean and adventurous breed, priding themselves on their fitness and despising the featherbedded Ups and the careful, corpulent Downs.

As for the Cellarmice, the rest thought nothing of them, regarding them as the lowest of the low. Cellarmice grew thick, coarse coats against the damp and chill of their subterranean quarters— coats that were always dark with coal dust. Shunned and snubbed by the other mice, they generally climbed out through gratings or via the coal chute to find their food in the farmyard or the farm buildings.

Rough and ready the Cellarmice may have been, but they were a cheerful lot, for they had something denied to the other three clans. As well as coal, there were barrels down there in the darkness. Every day the old farmer climbed down the cellar steps to draw himself a jugful of scrumpy, the hard cider made from small sweet apples, and every day the Cellarmice gathered afterward to drink the drops that he spilled and the drippings from the wooden spigot of the barrel and generally to have a good old time.

Mrs. Gray was an Attic of good birth. She had in fact been born in a nest of eiderdown in a discarded doll carriage that had once belonged to the now middle-aged daughter of the old farmer and his wife.

As expected, this wellborn doe had married an Attic buck, named Brown, and not long after given birth to seven lovely little Attics. Mr. Brown was the sort of young fellow who prided himself on being able to snatch cheese from traps without being caught. That pride came before his fall.

Once widowed, Mrs. Brown (as she was then called) had, during an expedition to the ground floor of the farmhouse, met a sleek and overfed Down named Mr. Black. She had fallen for him, but shortly after becoming the father of her next ten cubs, he had fallen into the fishtank.

Perhaps to drown her sorrows, the widow Black had immediately accepted the proposal of a rather elderly Up by the name of Gray.

This marriage, which resulted in the birth of the trins, was, for Mrs. Gray, filled with worry on account of her third husband's nearsightedness.

"Keep your eyes peeled for the cats," she would tell him each time he left home, but alas, the night came when poor Gray walked straight down a cat's throat.

"I saw it coming," said Mrs. Gray to the friend (a fellow Attic) who had brought the sad news.

"He didn't," said the friend. She regarded Mrs. Gray with a beady eye.

"If you don't mind my saying so, dear," she continued, "it all comes from marrying beneath you. Black was a Down, and even your late lamented was only an Up. Mixed marriages are always a gamble, I say. One of my next-door neighbor's girls has taken up with a Cellarmouse, if you please—a loudmouthed drunkard, my neighbor says he is. She's ever so worried for the grandchildren. In my view, dear, Attics should stick together."

"I told you," said Mrs. Gray a trifle sharply, "I'm not marrying again. My whole life will henceforth be devoted to the education and up-bringing of Thomas, Richard, and Henry. Of all the mice that have ever lived at Orchard Farm, my trins will be the most remarkable. Future generations will speak of them with awe and wonder.''

The friend snickered somewhat spitefully.

"Good grief!" she said. "What are they going to do, dear? Frighten the life out of the cats?"

"I shouldn't be at all surprised," said Mrs. Gray coldly.

3 SIX CATS

The cats of Orchard Farm were six in number. Four of these did not come into the house, but came only to the back door if and when old Mrs. Budge, the farmer's wife, put out a few scraps for them or a bowl of milk gone sour in warm weather. They were common, or farmyard, mousers and ratters, who patrolled barn and cowshed and granary.

The other two were house cats, tolerated by Farmer Budge (who disliked them and all their kind) just as long as they killed mice (which he disliked even more).

One was a pure-white tom, rather deaf (as are many of that color) but with sharp green eyes. Yellow, but no less sharp, were the eyes of the other, a black female. The white was named Wallace, the black, Bertha.

The four yard cats—all nameless tabbies—lived exclusively on the Cellarmice who came up and out from their dark dungeons.

These were especially easy to catch when they had had a drop too much scrumpy.

Wallace and Bertha caught no Cellarmice, the occasional Attic, and a few Ups, but the Downs were their principal prey.

This was the price the Downs paid for living close to food and warmth—and thus close to Wallace and Bertha, who seldom ventured upstairs.

Poor Mr. Gray had met his end in the kitchen, not noticing black Bertha in the darkness. Perhaps because it had been so pathetic, Mrs. Gray had felt the loss of her third husband more keenly than that of Brown or Black.

She addressed the trins, sleeping peacefully in their nest. "Cats!" she said. "We don't stand a mouse in hell's chance against them."

Then she remembered her friend's recent sarcastic remark. How wonderful it would be if when Thomas, Richard, and Henry were grown up, they really could somehow "frighten the life out of the cats"! What a revenge that would be for the death of the trins' father!

At that instant Mrs. Gray made a decision. She would train the trins to become guerrilla fighters in the cause of mousedom.

They would not grow up timid and fearful like other mice, but bold and cunning and ingenious, dedicated to waging unceasing war on those two monsters, one white, one black, that ruled the farmhouse.

Not only Attics but also Ups and Downs would view them as heroes and saviors of mousekind. Even the despised Cellarmice would drink to the health of the terrible trins.

With this ambition in mind, Mrs. Gray set to work.

As soon as the trins' eyes were open and they were properly clothed in fur coats (grayish, as it turned out), their mother began to brainwash them.

"You are the greatest," she would croon as she lay and nursed them in the nest. "There have never been mice like you before. Remember, Thomas. Remember, Richard. Remember, Henry. You are the Terrible Trins." She even made up a special nursery rhyme, which she taught them to sing in their piping little voices.

Have you heard the news, puss?
There's trouble on your track.
So mind your *P*'s and *Q*'s, puss,
And never turn your back.
Who will make you pay, puss,
For all your many sins?
Who'll haunt you night and day, puss?
The Trins! The Trins! The Trins!

As soon as Thomas and Richard and Henry were old enough to leave the nest, Mrs. Gray started them on a fitness program.

At first it was quite modest—a series of running, jumping, and climbing exercises, all done in the attic. But before long she took them down into the upstairs, then on to the downstairs, training them to follow her at high speed along those many channels and tunnels and stairways, until they knew their way all over the old farmhouse.

Because she had had plenty of milk to give them and because they were only three in number, the trins grew at a great rate and were already much bigger and stronger than other cubs their own age among the Attics or Ups or Downs. But throughout this training program Mrs. Gray took great care to steer clear of Wallace and Bertha.

She showed the trins a mousetrap and explained its workings (with special reference to the late Mr. Brown), and (remembering the late Mr. Black) she pointed out the perils of the tropical fish tank.

But not until Thomas, Richard, and Henry were cubs no longer, but teenagers (in weeks, that is) and fine specimens of young mousehood, did she show them the archenemy.

She picked on Wallace, reckoning that his deafness made him safer to use as a demonstration model.

Very early one morning she took the trins down the M1, as the main mouseway was known. The M1 was a vertical shaft that led directly out of the attic via the back wall of the Budges' bedroom and ended under the kitchen sink. From here a number of minor roads ran around the kitchen, and Mrs. Gray chose one that had an exit just above and to one side of the kitchen stove.

Motioning to the trins to follow, she crept out to the edge of a cupboard top, and together they looked down at the large white shape that lay on its side below, fast asleep.

"That," said Mrs. Gray, "is a cat."

"It's big," said Thomas.

"It's ugly," said Richard.

"It stinks," said Henry.

"Is that the one that ate our dad?" asked Thomas.

"No," said Mrs. Gray. "That was a black one. This white one's different from most cats because he's a bit deaf. That's why I'm talking in a normal voice—he can't hear me."

"Can't he hear anything at all?" asked Richard.

16

"Not much."

"Not if we shouted in his ear?" asked Henry.

"Oh, I daresay he'd hear that, all right."

The trins looked at one another.

"Have you heard the news, puss?" sang Thomas softly.

"Who will make you pay, puss?" sang Richard.

"Who'll haunt you night and day, puss?" sang Henry.

Then they ran down the cupboard door, lined up beside the ear of the sleeping Wallace, bent forward until their little snouts were almost in it, and with one voice and as loudly as they could, squealed *"Boo!"*

4 ENTER KEVIN

Hard of hearing Wallace may have been, but not *that* hard. To be woken from a deep sleep by a three-mousepower shriek right in his ear hole was a shattering experience, like having a sudden strong electrical shock.

In one convulsive movement the white cat shot straight into the air, then landed with flattened ears and poker-stiff tail, glaring all around him for the cause of so terrible a noise. But there was nothing to be seen in the kitchen. The only sounds—now too distant for Wallace to hear—were the excited squeaks and giggles of the Gray family as they scuttled back up the M1.

"Oh, Mom, that was fun!" cried Richard when they reached their attic home.

"*He* didn't think so!" Henry said, laughing.

"Can we do it again another day?" asked Thomas.

Not a bad idea, thought Mrs. Gray. Psychological warfare—maybe that's the way to deal with the white one. Keep giving him shocks like that and turn him into a nervous wreck.

"We'll see," she said. "You boys did well to make such a quick getaway. That's where training pays off, you see. Now then, line up! I want to see you do six lengths of the attic floor and back again. Touch the wall at each end before you turn. Ready, set, go!"

Old Mrs. Budge, lying awake in bed in the room below, heard the patter of tiny feet above her head and smiled.

Dear little pretties, she said to herself. I sometimes wish we didn't keep cats. Mice are nice, mice are. I like to see them about the place with their bright eyes and their big ears and their little whiskers twitching. And she lay very still so as not to wake her husband while the noise above was going on.

In the kitchen Wallace had been joined by Bertha, who came in through the cat door with a dark, hairy Cellarmouse, still alive, in her mouth. She laid it down on the floor and put a paw on it. "Those farm tabbies," she said. "They seem to

19

think all the mice from the cellar belong to them. I gave them a piece of my mind, I can tell you. 'Now, look here,' I said, 'I'll catch whatever mice I choose,' I said, 'inside the house or outside. Just because I'm one of the house cats,' I said, 'doesn't mean I can't hunt in your dirty old farmyard if I want to,' I said, 'so mind your manners.' Common as muck they are, that lot."

"What?" said Wallace.

"Wallace!" cried Bertha. "You didn't hear a word I said!"

She moved a step or two closer to him, taking her foot off her prey as she did so, and spoke more loudly.

"Whatever's the matter with you?" she said. "You're as white as a sheet."

"Had a shock," mumbled Wallace.

"What? Where? How? Why? When? What happened to you?" said Bertha.

"Nasty noise," said Wallace. "In my head. Woke me up. Startled me."

All this time the Cellarmouse that Bertha had caught was crawling dazedly away. It was very shocked and damp and disheveled from being car-

ried in the black cat's jaws, but it was unhurt. It headed for a mousehole under the bottom of the same cupboard on which the Grays had stood to look down on Wallace.

"A noise in your head?" said Bertha. "What nonsense, Wallace. You've had a nightmare, I expect, that's all it was. Have some of my mouse now and you'll feel better. I'll bite his head off and you can eat that—brains are very good for a shock, my old mother always told me."

But when Bertha looked around, the Cellarmouse had disappeared.

The black cat growled angrily.

"Now look what you've made me go and do," she hissed. "If you hadn't kept on and on, chattering away nineteen to the dozen about some stupid noise in your head, we could have shared that mouse, but as it is, he's scrammed, and it's all your fault, d'you hear me?"

"What?" said Wallace.

Without another word (surprisingly), Bertha flounced out the cat door.

Under the cupboard, the Cellarmouse sat shivering at the sound of the cats' voices, and not till they had ceased did he begin to pull himself together. He sat up and began to inspect himself for damage but could find none. All that was wrong with him (and it was bad enough) was that he had an awful headache, which had nothing to do with the cat.

What a fool I am, he said to himself, to have had so much to drink.

The previous night there had been quite a party in the cellar. In the evening Farmer Budge had come down to refill his cider jug. Going back up the dark cellar steps he had tripped and spilled quite a lot of cider.

A number of jolly young bucks had found the pool of scrumpy, and this particular Cellarmouse, whose name was Kevin and who was old enough to have known better, had joined them.

Determined to show that he could drink mouse for mouse with these youngsters, Kevin had downed drop after drop of the strong cider until his head was spinning.

"Shorry, chapsh," he muttered to the others. "I musht be going now."

"No, no, Kevin, old boy!" they cried. "Have one for the road."

So he did, before staggering up and out through a grating in search of fresh air.

Emerging into the farmyard as dawn broke, Kevin looked up to see two suns rising over the twin tops of two cowsheds. He shut his eyes and shook his head to clear it. When he opened his eyes again it was to see two black cats standing before him.

Now, peering out from the hole under the cupboard, he saw that there was a single white cat in what, he realized, must be the kitchen. I can't get out that way, he thought. How am I to get back down into the cellar?

At that moment he scented mice approaching along a runway somewhere in the wall behind him. And they won't be Cellarmice, he said to himself. They'll be Downs, or worse, Ups, or worse still, Attics, and they'll probably beat me up.

Oh, what a fool I am, he thought once more. I'll never touch the stuff again, I swear it. I'm sticking to rainwater from now on, if I ever get out of here in one piece, that is. Oh, dear, oh, dear, I am of all mice the most miserable.

And to the trins, who had just popped back down the M1 in search of breakfast, that was indeed how poor bedraggled hungover Kevin appeared.

5 DOWN WITH THE DOWN

At the sight of the three sleek, strong-looking young mice that confronted him, Kevin set his back against the wall and prepared to do his best against such odds.

"Keep away!" he cried. "I warn you, I am the light-heavyweight champion of the cellar!"

The trins looked doubtfully at this large, unkempt stranger who seemed so wretched and sounded so desperate. He was the first Cellarmouse they had ever met.

"Keep your hair on," said Thomas.

"Relax, mister," said Richard.

"Take it easy," said Henry. "We've got no quarrel with you. What's eating you, anyway?"

"A cat nearly did," said Kevin.

"A white one?" asked the trins.

"No, black. But I managed to escape. By the way, my name's Kevin."

"How do you do?" they said.

"Not very well, actually," said Kevin. "In fact,
what I really need is to lie down. But I can't think

how to get back to the cellar. I don't suppose you chaps know the way?"

"Afraid not," said Henry.

"Never been down there," said Thomas.

"We're Attics," said Richard. "I'm Richard Gray."

"And I'm Thomas Gray."

"And I'm Henry Gray."

"Brothers?" asked Kevin.

"Trins," they said.

Kevin didn't know what a trin was, but the three young mice appeared so friendly that he began to feel much happier. His headache was a bit better, too.

"My mother always told me that Attics were a stuck-up lot," he said, "but you fellows aren't like that."

"Our mom has a friend . . ." said Richard.

"Who always says . . ." went on Henry.

"That Cellarmice are the pits," finished Thomas.

At this Kevin once again looked woebegone, and the trins hastened to comfort him.

"Come on now, Kevin," said Thomas.

"Come and have some breakfast," said Henry.

"And afterward," said Richard, "we'll take you up to our place and introduce you to our mom."

Using a bypass, they led the way around the kitchen, finally emerging at the back of the pantry. This was a sizable room, its walls lined with shelves on which stood all manner of cans and packages and jars. On a great slab of slate stood a number of cheeses.

Already there were a good many mice at this breakfast table, mainly Downs, but with a sprinkling of Ups and Attics. What there were not, of course, nor ever before had been, were any Cellarmice, and at the sight of Kevin everyone stopped eating and stared at him with unfriendly beady eyes.

"Hey, you!" growled a big Down buck. "What d'you think you're up to? Get back where you belong and be quick about it, you dirty object."

"Excuse me," said Thomas politely. "He's our guest."

"We've invited him to breakfast," said Richard.

"Guest? Breakfast?" spluttered the big Down.

"What on earth do you mean? I don't understand."

"Hard cheese," said Henry, and there were some snickers among the listeners.

Stung by this, the big buck advanced threateningly toward Kevin.

"Out of my way, boys!" he snapped at the trins. "I'm going to teach this scruffy Cellarmouse a lesson."

But not for nothing had Mrs. Gray given her sons a thorough training in the martial arts.

"If you get into a fight, boys," she had said, "always remember—unity is strength. They say a good big 'un will beat a good little 'un, and that may be so. But the three of you together can beat the biggest of mice. Teamwork, that's the secret. Thomas—you go for his left ear. Henry—his right. Richard—fasten on the root of his tail. Get a good grip, each of you, and pull hard. And don't waste your breath name-calling or threatening your opponent—none of this 'Say that again and see what you'll get' stuff. Speed and surprise is everything—go straight in, hard and fast. No mouse will stand a chance against an attack like that."

How right she was.

One moment the big Down was talking about teaching Kevin a lesson, the next he was receiving a very painful one himself.

With Thomas to the left of him, Henry to the right of him, Richard behind him, their jaws tightly clamped on each respective target area, he struggled helplessly in their grip.

"I give up! I give up!" he squealed, banging on the slate slab with his forepaws, and when they let him go, he fled, torn and bleeding. The spectators, aghast at the power of the terrible trins, fled with him.

The three Gray boys looked at one another with satisfaction.

"Unity . . ." said Thomas.

"Is . . ." said Richard.

"Strength," said Henry.

They turned to Kevin.

"Now then," said Thomas, "what will you have? Cheddar?"

"Or Double Gloucester?" said Richard.

"Or," said Henry, "there's a good Edam."

As a matter of fact, Kevin tried all three.

Unlike his usual rather boring diet—grains of

spilled corn or nibblings from the potato bin—the cheeses were delicious, and he stuffed himself.

So full was he afterward that it was only with great difficulty that he managed to follow the trins up the M1 to the attic.

"Wait for me, chaps!" he called plaintively as they scampered ahead up the steep shaft, and by the time he reached the end of the mouseway he was so exhausted—by all his adventures, by his huge breakfast, and by the remains of his hang-over—that he sank down on the attic floor and closed his eyes.

Dimly he heard one of the trins saying "Mom, this is Kevin. Kevin, this is Mom." He opened one eye again. Then he opened both, wide. Then he struggled to his feet before the lovely Attic lady.

Oh, thought Kevin, the beauty of the world! The paragon of animals!

"Good morning, Mr. Kevin," said Mrs. Gray graciously. "The boys have been telling me all about you. I do hope you are feeling better now?"

Kevin gulped.

"Oh, yes, Mrs. Gray, thank you," he said. "Much, much better."

6 CAT BAITING

First thing every morning old Mrs. Budge would go to her pantry to clean up after the mice. There would be lots of nibble marks around the hard cheeses and little footprints in the soft cheeses, and mouse droppings everywhere on the slate slab, all things that Farmer Budge must never be allowed to see.

"He'd go mad," said Mrs. Budge, "if he knew what my little pretties get up to." And she carefully pared off all the mouse-chewed pieces and set them aside. By the end of the week there would be enough of them to make her husband cheese on toast for his supper.

One thing you can say for Budge, she often thought, is that he's easy to feed. The farmer's favorite breakfast, or any other meal for that matter, was a pint of cider and some bread and cheese.

When Farmer Budge had finished the milking that morning, he came into the kitchen as usual (without removing his boots) and sat down at the table (without washing his hands). Mrs. Budge set before him a loaf of bread, a large wedge of cheese, and two pint glasses. One was filled with scrumpy, one with water.

Then with his thumb and forefinger the farmer reached up and took out his right eye (it was made of glass) and dropped it into the glass of water.

After a good swig of cider, he took from his pocket a huge jackknife, cut off a great hunk of

bread, cut off a great hunk of cheese, and shoved both into his mouth. He chewed away with his mouth wide open, washing down every mouthful with more cider, watched by the glass eye, which stared balefully up at him from its watery lodging.

Wallace and Bertha were always wary of a kick from Farmer Budge—especially Wallace, who often did not hear him coming. But this morning Mrs. Budge noticed that the white cat seemed especially jittery. He kept jumping up and staring anxiously around the kitchen.

"What's up with our Wallace?" said Mrs. Budge.

Her husband fixed the white cat with his one good eye.

"Cats!" he said. "I hates 'em."

He drained his glass of scrumpy and wiped his mouth on one sleeve. Then he picked out the eye from the other glass, dried and polished it on his other sleeve, and popped it back into its socket.

"Only one thing I hates more than cats," he said, "and that's mice." And he stomped out.

Mrs. Budge shook her head sadly.

"Poor old Wallace," she said, and she bent to stroke him. "What's the matter?"

But Wallace jumped at her touch and stalked away, his tail swishing.

"You're like Budge this morning," she said. "Got up on the wrong side of the bed."

"Bed," said Mrs. Gray firmly, up in the attic. "That's the place for you, Mr. Kevin. You say you're feeling better, but you've had a nasty shock. Rest, that's what you need."

Kevin was embarrassed. Here he was, a mere Cellarmouse, up in the attic, and what's more, being offered a bed by this lovely Attic lady.

"Oh, no, no," he muttered. "I know my place. If you could just direct me back down to the cellar, Mrs. Gray, I won't take up any more of your time."

"No hurry, Kevin," said Thomas.

"We'll take you back down later," said Richard.

"You have a nap first, like Mom says," added Henry.

"We have plenty of spare rooms," said Mrs. Gray.

In fact, the Gray family lived inside an old discarded wing chair that had stood in the attic for many years. Generations of mice had used it before the Grays, each making alterations and improvements, so that its stuffing was honeycombed with holes and passages and comfy little nests. Mrs. Gray's rooms were in the back of the chair, the trins lived in the seat, and the wings were kept for visitors.

Kevin looked at his three new young friends and their beautiful mother, and the thought of returning to the dark, dank cellar suddenly seemed rather unattractive.

"Well, if you're sure," he said. "I do feel a little tired."

"All right, boys," said Mrs. Gray briskly. "Put Mr. Kevin in the west wing."

Well fed, warm, and comfortable, Kevin slept long and soundly.

When at last he woke and emerged from his room, he could see no sign of the Grays.

"Anyone at home?" he squeaked, but there was no answer.

At the sound of his voice a number of Attic

came from distant corners and crevices to take a look at this, the first Cellarmouse ever to reach such heights. News travels with the speed of light in a mouse colony, and already everyone knew what had happened that morning. Their instinct, as Attics, was to rush at this interloper and drive him back down where he belonged. But they all had heard the story, which had grown somewhat in the telling, of how the amazing Gray trins had practically killed a giant Down buck in defense of this particular Cellarmouse, and no one wanted to risk a similar fate. Only Mrs. Gray's friend's next-door neighbor (the one whose daughter had run away with a cider-swilling Cellarmouse) was bold enough to hiss "Boozer!" at him as she scuttled by.

At this point Mrs. Gray appeared from the top exit of the M1.

"Did you have a nice nap?" she asked.

"Oh, yes, thanks," said Kevin. "I really must be going now. If your boys wouldn't mind showing me the way?"

"I'm afraid you'll have to wait a little while," said Mrs. Gray. "They're busy just at the moment."

"Oh," said Kevin, "what are they doing?"

"Cat baiting," said Mrs. Gray.

A second assault on the white cat must be made that same day, she had decided. The shocks to his system must be frequent.

"You've got to keep at him, boys," she had told the trins. "Every time he drops off, in you must go. Jangle his nerves, never give him any peace."

And so once Kevin was settled in the west wing, Mrs. Gray had led the trins down to the kitchen and told them to keep watch on Wallace. She found them a suitable observation post—a mousehole at floor level. It was not far from the stove, whose warmth the cats usually slept beside, and it had a good escape route back to the M1.

"Take shifts," she said. "One hour on, two off. The moment he's fast asleep whoever is on watch wakes the others. Then it's off like a flash. All together, yell in his ear and back up out of sight before he knows what hit him."

"Piece of cake, Mom," they said. "Tell Kevin we'll be back soon."

But each of them had stood his hour's watch

before the white cat relaxed enough to go back to sleep again.

Richard, who was on guard at the time, woke Henry and Thomas, and they slipped out of the mousehole.

"All together," he said.

"Yell in his ear," said Henry.

"And back up out of sight," said Thomas.

And away they went.

This time the *"Boo!"* they gave into the depths of Wallace's ear was even louder than their first attempt. So loud was it, in fact, that it drowned out the squeak of the cat door as black Bertha slipped into the kitchen.

7 EXIT WALLACE

Old Mrs. Budge came out of the pantry, where she had been cutting off a large wedge of cheese for her husband's lunch, in time to see Wallace leap up with a yowl of horror at the awful noise sounding—for the second time—inside his head. He dashed past her and through the door that led to the living room, where he hid under the sofa.

The farmer's wife saw that there were three mice huddled together on the kitchen floor, staring pop-eyed at the black cat crouched in front of them. Oh, poor little pretties, she thought.

Mrs. Budge did her best for the mice of Orchard Farm. Though she had not been able to save Mrs. Gray's first husband, she always hunted for the mousetraps that Farmer Budge set all over the farmhouse, and when she found one she would spring it.

Usually there was no way she could stop the cats from killing mice, but here was a chance to do so. She prepared to hurl the lump of cheese at Bertha.

At that very moment Farmer Budge came through the back door for his midday meal. He carried his cow-whacking stick and was followed by his collie, Nip, who disliked cats even more than his master did. In an instant all was chaos.

Farmer Budge shouted "Mice!" and struck at the trins with his stick, missing them.

Mrs. Budge cried "Scat!" and threw the cheese at Bertha, hitting her.

With a growl, Nip charged at the black cat, who leaped on the kitchen table, upsetting the jug of scrumpy that was put there for the farmer's lunch, before disappearing at top speed.

The spilled cider dripped down on Thomas, Richard, and Henry Gray before they whisked into the safety of the mousehole.

As they sped back up the M1 they could hear a hubbub of loud, angry voices below.

While Mr. and Mrs. Budge were shouting at

each other, Nip quietly ate the wedge of cheese.

"What's all that noise downstairs?" asked Mrs. Gray when the trins reached home. "What have you boys been up to?"

She sniffed at them.

"And whatever do you smell of? Do you know what it is, Mr. Kevin?"

"Alas, only too well, Mrs. Gray," said Kevin. "Strong drink is raging," he added sadly.

"What do you mean?" asked Mrs. Gray.

"Your sons have been at the cider. I should have warned them against the evils of alcohol," said Kevin. "You lads have been down in the cellar, haven't you?"

"No, we haven't, Kevin," they said, and they described everything that had happened.

Kevin listened in amazement.

"Shouting in a cat's ear?" Kevin said. "I can't believe it. Mice just don't do that sort of thing."

"My trins do," said Mrs. Gray proudly. "But," she added, "we've got to be more careful, boys. You nearly got killed, by the sound of things. Next time you go after the white cat, I'm coming with you to act as a lookout."

"Okay, Mom," they said.

"No, no," cried Kevin. "You must not expose yourself to such danger, Mrs. Gray! Allow me to go in your place, I beg of you."

The trins' mother looked in surprise at the large, hairy Cellarmouse.

"I thought you were eager to return home, Mr. Kevin," she said.

How wrong you are, thought Kevin. I'm only eager to stay here by your side. Even if it means volunteering to fight in a war against cats.

"I would like to help," he muttered.

"Let him, Mom," said Richard. He began to groom his coat, damp from the spilled cider. "Hmm," he said, "not bad."

His brothers followed suit.

"Tastes nice," said Henry, swallowing.

"Perhaps," said Thomas, licking his lips, "we'd better take Kevin back down to the cellar after all!" And all three trins giggled.

"No," said Mrs. Gray firmly. "I think we should accept Mr. Kevin's offer. We can do with all the help we can get in our crusade. Don't forget that when we've defeated the white enemy, we've still got to deal with the black one."

Oh, no, thought Kevin. What have I done?

He found out that very evening.

As soon as the trins had finished licking the

cider splashes off themselves, Mrs. Gray ordered everyone to bed. Thomas, Richard, and Henry were not sorry to put their heads down, for oddly enough they suddenly felt rather sleepy. As for Kevin, he would have jumped out the attic window if Mrs. Gray had commanded it.

Once he was settled in the west wing and the trins were asleep in the chair seat, Mrs. Gray set off to locate the white cat. She did not travel by the mouseway. Instead she moved by minor roads down through the region of the Ups and finished up in the region of the Downs. She went slowly and carefully, keeping to the left, and she did not speak to any strange mice. There was not much traffic anyway, since it was still some time before rush hour.

Methodically she checked each of the downstairs rooms, noting the position of a number of newly set mousetraps that were hidden in various places, until at last she found Wallace.

He was still under the sofa in the living room, lying on his stomach, his head between his forepaws, in the deep sleep of nervous exhaustion. By a happy chance, Mrs. Gray saw, one of the fresh mousetraps had been set beneath the sofa, not three feet from the end of his white tail.

Back up the fast lane of the M1 she went at top speed.

Quickly she woke the trins and Kevin and outlined her plan of attack.

"We'll have to hurry," she said, "before he wakes up. Now, do you all understand what to do?"

"Sure, Mom," said the trins.

"Yes, Mrs. Gray," said Kevin. It's a crazy idea, he said to himself as they scuttled down the mouseway. I shall be killed and eaten for sure.

Mrs. Gray's scheme was indeed a dangerous one. Yet for all her talk about being careful, she thought the risks worthwhile. This was too good a chance to be missed. Never again were they likely to find a sleeping cat (and a rather deaf one at that) and a newly set mousetrap so close together.

The first thing to do was to move the trap within range. No mouse could have shifted it alone, but between the five of them they nosed it carefully and gently forward, sliding it along inch by inch until it was right beside that limp white tail.

46

"Now then," whispered Mrs. Gray, "take your places, everyone." With Thomas she crept up to Wallace's right ear while Richard and Henry stationed themselves by his left. Kevin, shaking with fear, placed himself just beyond the edge of the sofa, about six mouse-lengths from the sleeping cat.

They waited.

In a moment or two Wallace's senses reacted to the strong scent of mouse in the air, and his green eyes opened wide. There was one of the creatures sitting and staring at him, a big dark hairy one. Impudent little beast!

"You mustn't run the moment he sees you, Mr. Kevin," Mrs. Gray had said in her briefing. "You must try to keep still until he gets mad at you. Otherwise it won't work."

And somehow Kevin managed to stay where he was long enough for Wallace's tail to begin to swish and thump as angry cats' tails do.

Then everything happened at once, just as Mrs. Gray had hoped it would.

The mousetrap suddenly snapped shut on the tip of that swishing tail while the Grays squealed as loudly as they could into the depths of Wal-

lace's ears. Then as Kevin dodged out of the way, the white cat shot out from beneath the sofa with a screech of horror and the trap bouncing behind him.

Safely back in the attic, the cat baiters sat in the old wing chair savoring victory.

"Did you see him run!" said Thomas.

"Did you hear him yell!" said Richard.

"Laugh!" said Henry. "I thought I would die!"

I thought *I* would die, Kevin said to himself, and he felt very pleased that he hadn't.

"It all worked out beautifully, didn't it?" said Mrs. Gray. "He'll have a tailache to go with his headache. But we couldn't have done it without the help of our friend here."

She turned to the Cellarmouse.

"Thank you, Mr. Kevin," she said. "You stood your ground mousefully."

Kevin's heart swelled within his bosom.

"Actually," he said, "my full name is Kevin Coaldust. But please, Mrs. Gray, couldn't you drop the 'Mister'?"

"Yes, why don't you, Mom?" said the trins. "Just call him Kevin, like we do."

"If you wish," said Mrs. Gray demurely.

She made her way up to a hole in the back of the wing chair.

"I think I'll take a nap," she said. "So good night, boys."

" 'Night, Mom," said the trins.

"And good night, er, Kevin."

"Sleep well, Mrs. Gray," said Kevin as she disappeared from view.

"Dolly," said Richard.

"I beg your pardon?" said Kevin.

"That's Mom's name," said Thomas.

"So why don't you stop calling her 'Mrs. Gray,'" said Henry, "and call her Dolly."

"Oh," said Kevin. "D'you really think I should?"

Thomas looked at Richard, and Richard looked at Henry, and Henry looked at Thomas.

"Yes," they all said. "We really think you should."

Dolly Gray, thought Kevin. What a nice name. But how much nicer if it was Dolly Coaldust.

8 MRS. PRY PRIES

Never again did the white cat Wallace set foot inside Orchard Farm.

The mousetrap soon dropped off his tail, and the bruise it had made quickly healed, but Wallace's nerves had been frazzled by those continual shrill mysterious noises inside his head.

For a while he wandered, lonely as a cloud, not thinking what he was doing or looking where he was going, until at last he found himself in the outskirts of the nearest town. Here his luck changed.

Feeling very hungry, he jumped on a window sill and meowed pitifully at the people he could see through the pane—two old ladies who loved cats and had always (believe it or not) wanted a white one with green eyes.

And so, happy now and well fed and cosseted

for the rest of his days in a totally mouseless house, Wallace disappears from the story of the terrible trins.

"Our Wallace has disappeared," said Mrs. Budge to her husband at lunch the next day.

"Good," said Farmer Budge.

He took out his eye and dropped it into the glass of water, where it leered at him wetly.

"Anyway," said Mrs. Budge, "we've still got our Bertha."

"Cats!" said Farmer Budge.

"Well, you don't like the mice."

"Mice!" shouted the farmer, striking out with his cow-whacking stick at an imaginary mouse. "I hates them! We've got the most cunningest mice in this house as ever was. They do spring nearly every trap I do set without getting caught. I don't know how they does it."

Behind her husband's back Mrs. Budge smiled.

"And another thing," said Farmer Budge. "Yesterday I put a trap under the sofa in the living room, and now it's gone, disappeared completely."

"What, the sofa?" said Mrs. Budge.

"No, the trap!" shouted the farmer, and once again he whacked the floor with his stick, narrowly missing Nip, who let out a startled yelp.

"Stupid dog!" said Farmer Budge, and he filled his mouth with bread and cheese and poured in a lot of scrumpy as he was chewing.

Oh, Budge, Budge, thought his wife. What a man you are for dislikes. You can't stand cats nor mice nor the dog nor me. The only things you like are your cheese and your cider. Oh, and that old eye.

And it was true. Farmer Budge's eye meant a great deal to him. He was attached to it, you might say—except at mealtimes when he took it out. This he also did at night, putting it in a tooth glass by his bedside. He never cleaned his teeth, but the precious eye was a different matter, and he always added a drop of gin to the water in the tooth glass. This, he reckoned, was excellent stuff for glass-eye cleaning, and once the eye was put back in the morning, he drank the mixture.

Now, the bread and cheese finished, he drained his glass of scrumpy and stomped out of the kitchen, leaving large cow-dungy footprints across the floor.

While Mrs. Budge was mopping these up, the black cat came and rubbed against her, purring.

"You'll miss our Wallace, anyway, won't you, our Bertha?" said Mrs. Budge, but the answer sounded strangely like "Nee-oh."

Already the news of Wallace's departure had reached Mrs. Gray's ears. A harvest mouse had seen him wandering away and had told some long-tailed field mice, and they in turn had passed the tidings on to a foraging Cellarmouse. From down there a Down had heard it and had passed it up to an Up, who had mentioned it to an Attic, by chance none other than Mrs. Gray's friend.

She was not slow to seek out the trins' mother.

For some time now it had been common knowledge that the widow Gray had a lodger staying in the old wing chair, and the gossipy Attic does had a fine time with this piece of news.

"A lodger?" said one. "Another doe, you mean, for company?"

"Oh, no," said a second. "No, no, no doe. It's a buck."

"Oh, a gentleman friend!"

"Oh, no, no gentleman. Would you believe it, he's a Cellarmouse!"

"Never!"

"Oh, yes. Ever so big, he is. And dark. And hairy."

"A real mouse's mouse, eh?"

"They're like that, those Cellarmice, I'm told: rough and tough."

"And talk about drinking—they never draw a sober breath!"

"To think! The late Mr. Gray was ever so refined. He'd be turning in his grave if he'd had one."

"Maybe they're just good friends."

"Oh, come on!"

And of course all were eager to find out more.

What better excuse for calling, thought Mrs. Gray's friend, than to bring the news about the white cat.

She hurried along to the wing chair and found Mrs. Gray sitting outside her nest in its seat, alone.

"Hello, dear," said the friend. "Long time no see."

"I'm afraid we've been busy," said Mrs. Gray.

Hmm, thought the friend.

"Your boys out, are they?" she asked.

"Yes, they've gone down to play with some Ups."

"On your own, then?" said the friend.

At this point Kevin poked his head out of the west wing.

Separate bedrooms at any rate, thought the friend.

"Introduce me, dear," she said.

"Oh, sorry," said Mrs. Gray. "Kevin, this is an old friend, Mrs. Pry. Meet Kevin Coaldust."

"Coaldust?" said Mrs. Pry. "I don't think I know any Attics by that name."

"You wouldn't," said Mrs. Gray.

"You're an Up, are you, Mr. Coaldust?" asked Mrs. Pry.

"No," said Kevin.

"A Down, then?"

"No," said Kevin. He suddenly decided he didn't care much for Mrs. Gray's friend.

"I'm a Cellarmouse born and bred," he said. "Any objections?"

Despite herself, Mrs. Pry felt a little thrill at

being spoken to this way. What a he-mouse he is, she thought.

"Oh, no," she said hastily. "No offense meant, I'm sure."

"What did you want?" said Mrs. Gray.

"What's that, dear?" said Mrs. Pry. "Oh, yes, goodness me, I was forgetting. I came to tell you the news. The white cat's gone."

"She didn't seem a bit surprised," Mrs. Pry told

the other Attic ladies later. "It was almost as though she was expecting it."

"But did you meet the lodger?" they all asked.

"Oh, yes," sniffed Mrs. Pry. "Can't think what she sees in him. Not my type at all. Still, you know what they say—one mouse's meat is another mouse's poison."

"I'm afraid I spoke a bit sharply to your friend," said Kevin when Mrs. Pry had left.

"Won't do her any harm," said Mrs. Gray. "She's a pokenose."

She sat up to arrange her whiskers, and Kevin thought how ravishing she looked.

"Could you go and find the boys?" she said. "I think we all ought to have a talk. Would you mind?"

In the nick of time Kevin stopped himself from saying "Not at all, Mrs. Gray." Now or never, he thought.

"Not at all, Dolly," he said.

Mrs. Gray stopped her grooming and stared at him for a moment. Then, "Thank you, Kevin," she said, and she went back to tidying her whiskers once more.

Told the news by Kevin, the trins came tumbling up in high spirits.

"One cat gone!" shouted Thomas.

"And one to go!" cried Richard.

"And then," said Henry, "there won't be a cat in the house!"

"There are four out in the farmyard," said Mrs. Gray.

"Yes," said Henry, "but we don't go out there."

"And they don't come in here," said Richard.

"They only ever catch Cellarmice," said Thomas.

"Thanks a bunch," said Kevin.

"Oh, sorry, Kev!" they said. "We don't think of you as a Cellarmouse. You're our friend. You're one of the family."

Wish I was, boys, thought Kevin. Wish I could become your stepfather.

"Quiet down, you three," said Mrs. Gray. "We may have won a battle, but we haven't won the war. That black cat is far more dangerous than the white one ever was. We won't be able to go and yell in her ear when we feel like it. We have to make a plan to deal with her."

"We'll make her pay!" said Thomas.

"For what she did to us," said Henry.

"Why, what did she do?" asked Kevin.

"Ate our dad," said Richard.

Oh, my! thought Kevin. And here's me wanting to be their stepfather. Is that a step in the right direction?

9 OPERATION GO-CAT

"You look worried, Kevin," said Mrs. Gray.

"Me?" said Kevin. "Oh, no. I was just thinking."

"You got a plan, Kev?" said the trins.

He hadn't, of course. There was only one thing on his mind, and that was that awful black cat. He remembered its gleaming teeth and its hot breath and the dreadful feelings of helplessness and hopelessness as he lay in its jaws.

How could this crazy Gray family possibly defeat such an enemy alone? They could not kill it. They could not drive it from the house as the white cat had been driven, as this black one must somehow be driven—but by whom? The dog? No, the cat would be too quick for it. The farmer's wife? No, she seemed to like all the animals. The farmer, then? He didn't seem to like anybody or anything except his cheese and his cider. If only he could somehow be persuaded to dislike the black cat even more than he now did.

"The farmer," Kevin said out loud.

"What about him?" said the Grays.

"If we could somehow get him on our side," said Kevin.

"Fat chance!" cried the trins.

"Surely, Kevin," said Mrs. Gray, "you must know how the man hates mice. Think of all the traps he sets."

"What I meant," said Kevin, "was that if we could only fix it so that the black cat became very unpopular with the farmer, he might kick it out of the house and never let it back."

"But how could we do that?" asked the trins.

"Well," said Kevin, "d'you remember that time you told me about, when the dog chased the cat and the cat knocked over the jug of cider and some of it splashed on you boys?"

"Of course!" said Thomas.

"A lovely drop of scrumpy!" said Richard.

"Scrummy-yummy-yum!" said Henry.

"And then you said that the farmer got very

angry because his drink had been spilled. Well, supposing the cat did that a second time. He'd get even angrier with it."

"But we couldn't make the cat jump on the table," said Mrs. Gray.

"Oh, yes, we could," said Kevin. "If there was a mouse on it. Just imagine—the farmer comes in for his meal, the jug full of cider is on the table, a mouse runs past the cat and up the table leg and hides behind the jug, the cat jumps onto the table, the mouse dodges, the cat leaps, the jug goes over, *crash*. Why, the farmer would go crazy if that happened again. He'd murder that cat!"

"Yes," said Mrs. Gray, "but that cat might murder that mouse. It would take a very brave mouse to act as a decoy like that."

It would, thought Kevin, but luckily, Dolly, you have three very brave sons.

"It would," he said. "Which of you boys is going to volunteer?"

Thomas looked at Richard, and Richard looked at Henry, and Henry looked at Thomas.

Then with one voice they cried "Unity is strength!"

"You mean you all want to do it?" said Kevin.

"We mean," said the trins, "that none of us wants to."

"It's your crackbrained scheme," said Henry.

"So if anyone's going to run past the cat and climb up onto the table . . ." said Richard.

"It's you, Kev," said Thomas. And off they ran, squeaking with laughter.

"Naughty boys," said Mrs. Gray. "Of course you couldn't be expected to take such a risk, Kevin, now, could you?"

Kevin swallowed.

"Oh, yes, Dolly," he said thickly. "I could."

It was not in Mrs. Gray's nature to go about anything halfheartedly, and she immediately set to work planning the scheme, which she codenamed Operation Go-Cat.

The first thing to be done, she decided, was to get Kevin fighting fit.

"Speed and agility," she told him. "That's what you're going to need, and frankly you're carrying too much weight at the moment."

So she handed him over to the trins.

"You boys know all about fitness now," she

64

said, "so get cracking on Kevin. Start with a little jogging and move on gradually to speed work. Up the wall, mind you, as well as on the floor. He's got to be able to climb that table leg like lightning."

"Don't worry, Mom," said Richard.

"When we're done with him," said Thomas, "he'll be the fittest mouse there ever was."

"Ready to run for his life," said Henry.

Which is just what I will be doing, thought Kevin.

As the days passed, he very much regretted first, that he had ever thought of such a plan, and second, that he had agreed to act as the decoy. Still, whatever was going to happen to him couldn't be much worse than what he was now being made to do by the trins.

They began with push-ups. Just a few at first, but then they worked him up to twenty, thirty, fifty, until Kevin's legs ached agonizingly and the effort of raising his heavy body from the floor was torture.

"Oh, not again, boys, please!" he would pant, but in vain.

"Feel the burn, Kev, feel the burn!" they chorused. And after that, when he already felt exhausted, he was made to jog and sprint and jump and climb, until at last Thomas or Richard or Henry would say "Okay, Kev. That'll do for now. Take five."

But it worked.

The new Kevin was not only slimmer but also much faster and more agile than the old, and Mrs. Gray, watching the training program with interest, decided to begin the next stage of Operation Go-Cat.

This took the form of a rehearsal.

It had to be done at night, of course (and at a time when Bertha was absent from the kitchen), which meant that there was no cat to chase Kevin and no cider jug to be knocked over, either. The point was to see how quickly Kevin could dash across the floor, shinny up the table leg, dodge between the two glasses—one full of scrumpy, one full of water and the glass eye—and hide behind the jug.

The Grays played the various parts. Mrs. Gray pretended to be Bertha, Thomas and Richard ere the two glasses, and Henry was the jug.

Time and again Kevin was made to come out om a hole (the same mousehole the trins had sed to hide in before), sprint past Mrs. Gray's ose, shoot up the table leg, and rush between homas and Richard to hide behind Henry.

At last Mrs. Gray pronounced herself satisfied.

"Well done, everybody," she said. "Boys, ou've done a good job in getting Kevin to peak ness. I'm proud of you."

What about me? thought Kevin. Don't I get any aise?

And as though she had read his mind, Mrs. ray said, "And tomorrow, Kevin, I'm sure I'm ing to be proud of you."

Kevin gulped.

"Tomorrow, Dolly?" he asked. "You mean . . ."

"Yes," said Mrs. Gray. "D day for Operation -Cat."

At lunchtime the following day the stage as set.

Kevin was in the mousehole waiting, the Grays ered from various other mouseholes around the chen, the cat lay before the stove, the farmer sat in his chair, and Mrs. Budge set before him the bread and cheese, the two glasses, and the cider jug.

Last of all, Farmer Budge took out his right eye and dropped it into the glass of water. Then he picked up the other glass and the jug and proceeded to fill one from the other.

At that instant Kevin burst out of the mousehole and dashed past the cat's nose and up the table leg, only to find that there was nowhere to hide but behind the glass of water. Desperately he dodged behind it and crouched down while the eye stared horribly at him.

Seconds later Bertha jumped onto the table and, lashing out at the cowering Kevin, knocked over the glass of water.

As the four Grays watched from their ringside seats, Kevin took a flying leap off the tabletop in one direction, the cat in another, while the glass fell to the floor and smashed to pieces.

Unseen by anybody, the glass eye rolled across the floorboards beneath the table until it chanced upon a knothole. Down through this it fell and disappeared from sight.

10 NOSEBALL

"Blast that cat!" shouted Farmer Budge. "Where's it gone?"

"Out through the cat door," said his wife.

"No, my eye! Where's my eye gone?"

"Eat your food," said Mrs. Budge. "I'll find it for you."

But when she got down on her hands and knees to sweep up the broken pieces of glass with a dustpan and brush, the eye was nowhere to be seen.

Budge will go mad, she thought.

"I can't find it," she said. "It's disappeared."

"*Aaargghh!*" yelled the farmer.

Budge *has* gone mad, she thought.

"That cat!" he shouted. "She must have taken it! She took my eye! I'll murder her, see if I don't!" And snatching up his gun from a corner, he blundered out of the room.

In a little while Mrs. Budge heard a loud bang.

"That's the end of our Bertha," she said sadly.

In fact it wasn't, for on account of having only one eye, Farmer Budge was a rotten shot. But it *was* the end of Bertha's time in the farmhouse, just as the Grays and Kevin had hoped.

First the farmer nailed a plank of wood over the cat door. Then he told his wife that she was never to allow the black cat to set foot inside the house again.

Then he did his best to make sure that it never set foot anywhere again.

Gun in hand, a black patch over his empty eye socket, he stalked around the farmyard, firing at anything that looked like Bertha (which included the four farm tabbies when the light was bad).

He didn't hit a single cat, but he scared the living daylights out of the five of them, so that they all went off to live wild in the woods and never came back to Orchard Farm again.

The cats gone, Farmer Budge redoubled his attack on the mice.

He bought more mousetraps and set them everywhere, and he bought packets and packets of poison and put saucerfuls of the stuff all over the house, from cellar to attic.

Mrs. Budge did her best for the mice. When she was sure her husband was out of the way (milking times were safest) she sprang traps wherever she found them and threw the poison pellets on the fire.

Despite her efforts, a number of Attics, Ups, Downs, and Cellarmice kicked the bucket.

"Poor little pretties," she would say. "If only Budge was nice to mice."

Meanwhile, the glass eye lay gathering dust under the kitchen floorboards, until one day the trins chanced upon it.

They had come down from the attic to scavenge under the kitchen floor. Here, because the farmer was a messy eater, there were often bread crumbs or even little bits of cheese rind that had fallen through cracks and holes in the boarding, and here they suddenly came upon the eye.

At first they did not recognize the round glass object but began instead to treat it as a plaything, rolling it about with their noses and playing a sort of game with it among themselves.

Not until they had rolled the dust off it did they see it for what it was, and then they shot up the M1 to report.

As they approached the old wing chair, the trins saw that their mother and Kevin seemed to be sitting rather close on the seat cushion, and Thomas nudged Richard, and Richard nudged Henry, and Henry nudged Thomas.

"What is it, boys?" said Mrs. Gray. "You look excited about something."

"We think we've found the farmer's eye," they said. "Come and see."

Down the mouseway they all scampered, and Kevin, who had after all been very close to it, confirmed that it was indeed the glass eye.

"Come on, Kev," said Thomas. "We've just invented a new game called noseball." And for a while he and Kevin played against Richard and Henry, dribbling the eye about with their snouts, while Mrs. Gray sat and watched and thought.

She was remembering that before Operation Go-Cat, Kevin had said of the farmer, "If we could somehow get him on our side." Surely the farmer

73

would be pleased if they could return his glass eye to him. But how?

Leaving the others to their game, she made her way back up the slow lane of the M1 to consider the matter.

No sooner had she gone than the glass eye disappeared from sight once again.

Kevin had made a determined run down the right wing, dribbling the ball—or the eye—strongly with his nose and brushing aside the tackles of first Richard and then Henry.

"Shoot, Kev!" squeaked Thomas, and with a

flick of his snout Kevin sent the ball whizzing across the playing floor, only to see it vanish down a hole.

"Oh, Kev!" cried the trins. "You've gone and lost our ball!" They peered down the hole.

"Where does this lead to?" they asked.

"It goes down to the cellar," said Kevin.

"We'll never get it back up," said Henry.

"Well, we can play down there," said Richard.

"Yes, let's go down after it," said Thomas.

"Better not," said Kevin.

"Why?"

"Well, the Cellarmice might not like you going down there."

"Because we're Attics, d'you mean?"

"Well, yes."

But the trins had no intention of losing their plaything or of giving up the newfound delights of noseball.

"We're going down anyway," they said, and they did.

Kevin followed reluctantly.

When they arrived, it was to see the glass eye in the middle of the cellar floor, surrounded by several curious Cellarmice, who looked at the four newcomers and recognized one of them.

"Why, if it isn't Kevin Coaldust!" said a voice.

"Thought you were dead," said another.

"Heard the cat got you."

"Where've you been?"

"Come and have a drink, Kevin, old buck."

There was a strong smell of cider in the air, and for a moment Kevin was tempted. But Dolly wouldn't approve, he thought, and anyhow, I don't want to lead her boys into bad ways.

"No thanks," he said.

"Please can we have our ball back?" said the trins.

"Your ball?" said the largest and toughest-looking of the Cellarmice.

"Yes," said Thomas. "Our ball."

"And be quick about it," said Richard.

"Or you'll be sorry," said Henry.

The big Cellarmouse swaggered toward them.

"And who might you be?" he said. "Uppity young Downs, I suppose?"

"No," they said.

"Ups, then?"

"No," they said.

"Don't tell me you're Attics?"

"Yes," they said.

"Well, well," said the big Cellarmouse. "Hoity-toity Attics, are you? Come to slum it among the lower classes, have you? Well, we've got no need of la-di-da young gentlemice down here, so why don't you get lost before I teach you a—" But before he could say any more, the three terrible trins came in hard and fast in their customary fighting formation: Thomas clamping on the Cellarmouse's left ear, Henry on his right, and Richard on the root of his tail.

"Sorry," said Kevin above the big Cellarmouse's squeals for mercy. "I should have warned you."

Respectfully the other Cellarmice drew back as their defeated gladiator dragged himself away.

Then they watched, fascinated, as the trins and Kevin began another game of noseball.

The space under the kitchen floorboards had not been level, but here the flat concrete surface of the cellar made a first-class playing field. To make matters even better, there were two barrels of cider at either end, and the space between each pair made an ideal goal.

"We really need goalies," panted Kevin after a while, and two young Cellarmice immediately volunteered.

Then others wanted to join in, and in no time at all they were playing five-on-five, watched by a crowd of other mice from all over the house who had heard about this new game of noseball and cheered loudly as the glass eye was trundled up and down the cellar floor.

When the game was over (Kevin and Thomas's team beat Richard and Henry's 4–3), there were plenty of others who wanted to play. Politely—for they knew the trins' reputation—they asked if they might borrow the ball, and a noseball tournament began.

Kevin organized it, Richard was the referee, and Henry and Thomas were the linemice.

First a team of Ups beat a team of Downs. Then the Attics played the Cellarmice and lost.

The final—Ups versus Cellarmice—was tied at the end of the game and had to be decided by a penalty shoot-out.

Thanks to a brilliant save by their goalie, an athletic young doe, the Ups won by one goal and were declared the champions.

Everyone agreed that noseball was great fun, even Mrs. Gray, who had come down the M1 to watch the final.

"But," she said to the trins when all but the Cellarmice had gone home, "we mustn't lose sight of that glass eye."

"Well, we can't take it up the mouseway, Mom," they said.

"Of course not, you silly boys. But it must be looked after very carefully."

She turned to Kevin. "I presume you have family living down here?" she said.

"Oh, yes," said Kevin. "In fact, that's my Auntie Ada over there."

"All right, then. It is your responsibility, Kevin, to see that no harm comes to the eye," said Mrs. Gray as she set off back to the attic.

"Yes, Dolly," said Kevin.

"Well!" said Kevin's Auntie Ada. "Fancy you being on first-name terms with a posh Attic lady like that! Known her long, have you?"

Kevin looked a little flustered.

"Quite a while, Auntie," he said.

"Well, well, well!" said Auntie Ada.

All eyes were on Kevin now.

Auntie Ada eyed him.

The other Cellarmice eyed him.

The trins eyed him.

Balefully, from the middle of the floor, Farmer Budge's glass eye eyed him.

Auntie Ada broke the silence.

"Why, Kevin Coaldust," she said, "I do believe you're planning to marry above yourself."

11 "POOR LITTLE PRETTY!"

"Don't know what the world's coming to," said Kevin's Auntie Ada as her nephew, who seemed embarrassed, disappeared up the mouseway. "A Cellarmouse courting an Attic! It wasn't like that in my young day."

"Don't see what's wrong with it," said Richard.

"What does it matter where anyone comes from?" said Henry.

"We're all mice, aren't we?" said Thomas.

"You youngsters don't understand," said Auntie Ada. "Every mouse should know its place in society. Our Kevin should be looking for a wife down here, where he belongs."

The trins looked around the cellar, where by now most of the inhabitants had gathered, and noticed a number of pretty young does.

"He certainly should!" they said, and the young does squeaked coyly.

"Anyway," said Thomas, "we must love you and leave you!" (at which there were more squeaks).

"And please," said Richard, "will you look after our ball for us?"

"Yes," said Henry. "Take good care of it, won't you?"

"Don't you worry, young gentlemice," said Auntie Ada. "Any friends of Kevin's are friends of all of us. Anyone who lays a paw on your property will have to answer to Ada Coaldust."

Meanwhile Kevin was speeding up the M1.

Gossip, he knew, spread like wildfire around Orchard Farm, and in no time at all everyone would have heard that he was not just boarding with the widow Gray but also had hopes of becoming her next husband.

He could just imagine Dolly's friend Mrs. Pry breaking the news. "A little bird told me, dear, that Kevin's about to pop the question!"

No, no, he must get there first. He must propose to Dolly Gray now, immediately!

He reached the top end of the mouseway and burst into the attic at full speed.

But even while Auntie Ada, at the bottom of the house, had been quizzing Kevin about his intentions, the farmer, at the top, had been setting fresh traps.

As Kevin rushed across the floor toward the old wing chair he heard Mrs. Gray's voice raised in urgent warning.

'Watch out, Kevin!" she cried. "There's a new—" And even as she uttered the final word "mousetrap" he saw it in his path. Unable to stop

in time, he leaped into the air in an attempt to hurdle it.

How nearly he succeeded, but alas, how narrowly and painfully he failed, for as he landed, one hind foot touched the pan of the trap, and with a horrid clack the metal arm snapped shut on his tail.

What a scene met the astonished eyes of the trins as they emerged from the M1.

In the center of the floor was a crowd of Attics, all pushing and shoving to get a look, just as people do at the scene of an accident. In the center of the crowd, they saw, was their friend Kevin, held tightly by the tail in a trap, while their mother stood helplessly by.

"Oh, Kevin, Kevin!" she was crying, and when she saw them, "Oh, boys, boys! Whatever can we do?"

"It's all right, Mom," they said, though they were shaken to see their mother, always so competent, at a loss. "It's all right."

"No, it's not," said Kevin. "It hurts like anything. And it's no good telling me to pull myself clear. I've tried, and the trap just follows me. I'm held fast."

And so he was, the trins could see—tightly gripped an inch or so from the tip of his tail.

"There's only one thing to do," said Henry

"Afraid so," said Thomas.

"The only question is," said Richard, "which of us is going to do it?"

"Do what?" said Mrs. Gray.

"Free Kev by biting through his tail," they said.

A shudder ran through the watching crowd, while Thomas looked at Richard, and Richard looked at Henry, and Henry looked at Thomas, and Mrs. Gray looked horrified.

Kevin gritted his teeth.

"Go on, then," he said. "One of you do it, quick, before the farmer comes back."

No sooner were the words out of Kevin's mouth than all the mice heard the sound of footsteps climbing the attic stairs.

In a flash every mouse except the wretched prisoner vanished from sight.

As the door creaked open and Kevin waited helplessly for death, one last regret filled his mind.

I never asked her to marry me, he thought, and now I never shall. He closed his eyes.

"Poor little pretty!" said a voice. "Don't be frightened, now. I'll soon have you out of there."

What celebrations there were in the attic that night!

To be sure, Kevin had a broken tail. (The final inch of which later dropped off. "He's so distinguished looking now," Mrs. Gray said when it did.) But he was alive, safe, and free!

And there was feasting, for Mrs. Budge had returned to the attic later with some cookies that she crumbled on the floor, to make up for the injury caused by her husband's horrid trap.

In the seat of the old wing chair sat the four Grays and Kevin, comfortably filled with cookies and happiness.

"Thank goodness," said Mrs. Gray, "that one of you boys did not have to bite through Kevin's tail."

She shuddered.

"Hear, hear!" said Kevin. "Actually, boys, how would you have decided who was the one to do it?"

"Eeny, meeny, miney, mo," they said.

"What I don't understand, Kevin," said Mrs. Gray, "is why you came rushing across the floor like that, so carelessly, not looking where you were going. Why ever were you in such a tearing hurry?"

Kevin scratched himself behind one ear with a hind foot, playing for time. This isn't quite how I planned it, asking her in front of the trins, he thought. Still, I suppose it concerns them. After all, I'll be asking to be their stepfather.

At that moment they heard a familiar voice from the floor in front of the chair. It was Mrs. Gray's friend.

"Are you there, dear?" called Mrs. Pry.

"No, Dolly, you're not," said Kevin quietly.

He stuck his snout over the edge of the chair cushion.

"Mrs. Gray is not at home," he said curtly.

"I could have sworn I heard her voice," said Mrs. Pry.

This was too much for Kevin, to be interrupted at such a moment and with a sore tail to boot.

"Oh, get lost, you nosy old bag!" he said.

"Kevin!" exclaimed Mrs. Gray as her friend departed in a huff, but she didn't sound all that displeased.

"Good old Kev!" said the trins. "But you still haven't said why you were in such a hurry."

"Because," said Kevin, "I was going to ask your mother something."

"It must have been very important," they said.

"It was," said Kevin. "It is. That's why I didn't want your friend around, Dolly."

"I see," said Mrs. Gray. "In that case, Kevin, hadn't you better ask me this very important question now?"

"Yes," said Kevin. "Will you marry me?"

12 THE FINAL

Farmer Budge had never been a good-tempered man. But since the loss of his precious glass eye, his ill nature had become much more marked. Now that there were no cats to shoot at, he had to be content with aiming a kick at Nip, or indeed at any farmyard creature—chicken, duck, or goose— that his one good eye fell on. As for the cows, in their twice-daily journey to and from milking, they received more than their fair share of whacks from the farmer's cow-whacking stick.

Worst off of all was Mrs. Budge. Her husband now never spoke to her without raising his voice in anger about anything and everything. The bread was not fresh enough, the cheese not tasty enough, the cider jug not full enough—nothing she did was right.

He even seemed to think it was somehow her

fault that he killed so few mice, for mostly they still sprang his traps without being caught, and as for the poison, it disappeared, apparently without harming them.

"Anybody'd think," he growled, "that you liked them."

"Liked who?" asked Mrs. Budge.

"The mice! The house is running with them."

"Well," said Mrs. Budge, "you've only got yourself to blame. Why our Wallace went I don't know, but it was you that drove our Bertha away."

"Course I did!" shouted the farmer furiously, tapping one dirty forefinger on the black patch he wore over his empty eye socket. "She took my eye, didn't she?"

If only I could find that eye, Mrs. Budge said to herself time after time. If only he had it back once more, I do believe Budge would be his old self again. Not that he was ever anything but an old grouch, but it would surely make him a bit happier to be able to pop it in and out again like he used to. Of course our Bertha never took it—whoever heard of a cat running off with a glass eye in its mouth? You might as well imagine the mice stole it! No, no, it's got to be somewhere about the place. I must take a really good look around for it.

But though she searched high and low, even finding the knothole through which (though she did not know it) the eye had originally fallen and taking up the floorboard to look beneath, she found nothing, of course.

"The darn thing's gone forever," said Mrs. Budge at last. But she was wrong.

One Sunday morning the trins had organized a knockout noseball competition. Usually the game was played at night, when the farmer and his wife were in bed and would not hear the squeaks of the crowd watching this new spectator sport on the cellar field.

But a Sunday mid-morning event, the trins decided, would be a good idea, since Mrs. Budge always went to church at that time and Farmer Budge would be fast asleep. On Sundays he always drank rather more cider than usual with his breakfast and then lay down on the sofa.

There were now a good number of noseball teams at Orchard Farm, so popular had the game become.

Attics by birth the trins may have been, but they made it quite clear to anyone and everyone that they much disliked the old snobbish clan system. Team members, they insisted, should be chosen for their skills and not on account of the floor of their birth. Thomas, Richard, and Henry Gray (who had, after all, invented the game) had Kevin and Kevin's Auntie Ada as the other members of their team. Thomas and Henry played on the wings, Richard was the forward, Kevin the defender, and Auntie Ada, who was very light on her feet for her age, was the goalie.

All the teams gave themselves fancy names, and the trins' was called Cellarattic United.

On this particular Sunday morning they had reached the final (to no one's surprise, for the Gray boys' nosework and ball control were outstanding) against the Updown Wanderers, in front of a large crowd.

Most of the mice of Orchard Farm had come to watch, though not the trins' mother, now Mrs. Coaldust.

"Aren't you coming, Mom?" they had asked.

"Not today, boys," Dolly said. "I think I'll sleep in."

"Not ill, Dolly dear, are you?" asked Kevin anxiously.

"No, no. Just a little queasy."

But on this particular morning, though the farmer was snoring as usual on the sofa, Mrs. Budge had not gone out. It was a very wet day, the rain coming down in bucketfuls, and she decided she'd miss church. Instead she made a nice cup of tea and treated herself to some cookies, taking care to scatter a few crumbs on the kitchen floor for her little friends.

Then she took up the empty cider jug to go and fill it, ready for her husband's lunch. The routine was always the same: Mrs. Budge fetched the scrumpy for the first two meals of the day, but when the afternoon milking was done, Farmer Budge himself went down to the cellar, drew a jugful for his tea, inspected the barrel in use to check its level—and do a little tasting while he was at it.

Mrs. Budge was neat and didn't spill a drop, but the clumsy farmer slopped the stuff everywhere. As a result, the evenings had always been the time for the Cellarmice to have a few drinks.

Thanks to noseball and the new chumminess

between the various clans, quite a few mice from all over the house now dropped in to enjoy the happy hour.

Jug in hand, her favorite old carpet slippers on her feet, Mrs. Budge tiptoed past her sleeping

94

husband and very quietly opened the door that led to the cellar.

She was halfway down the steps when she suddenly saw, by the light that came in through the gratings and the coal chute, a most extraordinary scene.

There below her, in the middle of a great crowd of spectators, ten mice were running about on the cellar floor, playing some kind of game with a round object that they pushed with their little snouts, while the onlookers squeaked encouragement. Very slowly, very quietly, Mrs. Budge descended another step or two to try to see what the object was. At that moment one of the players flicked the thing between two of the cider barrels amid loud squeals from the crowd.

Mrs. Budge could have had no idea that Richard Gray had scored the winning goal for Cellarattic United, beating the Updown Wanderers 3–2.

But she could see what he'd scored it with.

"Oh, my!" she breathed. "It's Budge's eye!"

13 ALL'S WELL...

The thoughts that now passed through Mrs. Budge's mind were the same as those that had earlier occurred to Dolly Coaldust.

If it could be made to seem that the mice had found Budge's precious eye, surely he would be bound to feel more kindly toward them?

Don't move, my pretties, she thought. Wait there while I go and fetch Budge. And she tiptoed back up the stairs.

Gently she shook her husband by the shoulder.

"Wake up," she said.

Farmer Budge opened his one good eye.

"Wassmarrer?" he said.

"I've got something for you," she said.

The farmer stared at the jug that Mrs. Budge was still carrying.

"The jug's empty," he said angrily.

"No, no," said Mrs. Budge. "It's something you lost. It's been found."

Farmer Budge struggled to his feet.

"My eye!" he shouted. "You've found my eye!"

"No, I didn't find it."

"Who did then? Nip?"

"No. It was my little pretties that found it for you."

"Pretties? What do you mean?"

"Come and see," said Mrs. Budge. "But hush, mind you, or you'll frighten them away."

Quietly the farmer in his stocking feet, his wife in her slippers, crept down the cellar steps.

As soon as the noseball final was over, the crowd of spectators had dispersed. Usually the regulars would get together for a few drops of scrumpy after a match, but last night's spillage had all been drunk.

The rainstorm over, the Cellarmice had gone out into the farmyard, which now, with no cats about, they could safely do in daylight.

The Downs, the Ups, and the Attics had all disappeared up the M1, leaving it at their various junctions.

Kevin had rushed ahead, before the mouseway became too crowded, anxious to see how his wife was feeling.

Only the trins remained behind.

They sat together in the middle of the cellar field, the glass eye beside them, savoring the pleasure of success. Cellarattic United were the champions!

"That last goal of yours was a great one, Richard," said Thomas.

"Couldn't have done it without you two," said Richard. "You gave Henry a perfect through pass, and he crossed it beautifully."

"Their goalie never had a chance," said Henry.

"Unity is strength," they all said happily.

"Kevin played a blinder," said Thomas.

"When old Kev tackles 'em, he tackles 'em," said Richard.

"And as for his Auntie Ada," said Henry, "she made some fantastic saves."

Thomas looked at Richard, and Richard looked at Henry, and Henry looked at Thomas.

"We are the greatest!" they cried.

All this time three eyes were watching them

from the cellar steps, until at last they ran away, leaving that fourth eye staring coldly at the farmer and his wife as they came toward it.

Farmer Budge bent down and picked it up. Still fuddled with sleep and his extra Sunday morning cider, he shook his head in bewilderment.

"I don't rightly understand," he said. "However did it get here?"

"I don't know," said Mrs. Budge, "but I reckon you've got the mice to thank for it. My little pretties found it somewhere, and they've brought it here for you. You saw them."

"Mice!" said Farmer Budge, but instead of shouting the word, he said it softly. "Well, I never!"

He stretched out his other hand.

"Here," he said, "give us that jug."

Then he turned the tap of the nearest cider barrel and filled the jug and took a long drink from it.

Then he pulled off his black eye patch and threw it away.

Carefully he washed the glass eye in the jug of cider, dried it on his sleeve, popped it back into its socket, and took another swig.

"How 'bout that!" he said, still quietly. "Them three little mice, finding my eye. I'll have to do summat about that."

"What will you do?" said Mrs. Budge.

"Stoke up the living room fire," said the farmer, "and you'll see."

How delighted the mice of Orchard Farm would have been to see what happened next. How delighted Mrs. Budge was.

For around the house went Farmer Budge, collecting all the poison baits and all the mousetraps. He then threw the lot onto the blazing fire. Finally, to Mrs. Budge's amazement, he even broke his cow-whacking stick over his knee and threw the two halves into the flames as well.

Old Mrs. Budge hugged herself for joy. Who'd have believed it, she thought. Budge is a changed man since he got his eye back.

So pleased was she that for the first time in many, many years, she used her husband's first name.

"Now then," she said, "I expect you're ready for your lunch, Ephraim."

Who knows, she thought, maybe he'll call me Eliza.

But all Farmer Budge said was, "Of course I am. Look sharp about it."

Talk about happy endings!

The cows were happier because they didn't get whacked as much. Nip and the hens and ducks and geese were happier because they didn't get so many kicks aimed at them.

Mrs. Budge was happier because Farmer Budge was, if not happy, at least not so grumpy and bad-tempered as before.

And the mice were happier because now all they had to die of was old age. Only one thing marred their happiness, and that was the loss of the glass eye. Now that they had no ball to play with, the noseball season ended abruptly—forever, it seemed.

The game's inventors, the trins, were especially miffed at the disappearance of their plaything.

"Just when the Cellarattic United were the league leaders," they said.

"The great thing is that all the traps and poison baits are gone," their mother said. "That's more important than your old noseball."

"Oh, Mom!" they said. "Just because you don't play."

"If your mother wished to play," said Kevin, "I'm sure she would be brilliant. But she cannot, at the present time."

"Of course she can't," they said. "We haven't got the glass eye anymore. None of us can play."

"Well, it's no good coming whining to me," said Dolly sharply. "Go and find something else to play the game with."

"Don't know what's up with Mom these days," the trins said to one another as they went off. "Anyone would think she's got something on her mind."

All the same, they spread the word around the house that if the game was to continue, a replacement ball must be found, and a number of keen young noseballers among the Attics, the Ups, and the Downs volunteered to go outside and join the Cellarmice in the search.

The first thing to be brought back was a smooth pebble from the garden path. But it was not perfectly round and wouldn't roll straight.

The next was an oak apple, but this was too light.

Then someone brought in a gooseberry from

the garden, but it was hairy and tickled their noses.

And a blackbird's egg, fallen from a nest unbroken, broke in the first head-on tackle and was quickly eaten by the players.

They even tried playing with small pieces of coal from the cellar, but they could never find one that would roll.

Farmer Budge of course knew nothing of the problems caused by the recovery of his eye, but Mrs. Budge did. She had taken to creeping halfway down the cellar steps to watch her little pretties at play, and it soon became clear to her that they needed help.

After some thought, she found in her bottom drawer an old necklace that she had not worn for many a year. It was made of a number of green glass globes of varying sizes, from little ones no bigger than peas to several that seemed to her about right.

She took one of these off the string, and, looking into the mirror, held it beside her own eye ("because I expect my eye's the same size as Budge's"), and it seemed exactly right.

What's more, she thought, there are two or three more like it to use as spares if they lose this one.

So it was with great delight that Thomas, Richard, and Henry Gray, coming down to the cellar for some practice, however unsatisfactory, with yet another old bit of coal, found waiting for them, in the middle of the cellar playing field, the green glass globe.

"Look at that!" squeaked Thomas.

"However did it get here?" squeaked Richard.

"Who cares!" squeaked Henry. "It's just perfect! We'll organize a tournament right away. Let's go and tell Kev!"

Pausing only to entrust the new ball in the care of Auntie Ada, they shot up the fast lane of the M1 to the attic.

"Kev! Kev!" they squealed. "Come down and see what we've got!"

From the seat of the old wing chair, Kevin looked over at the trins. His expression was smug.

"Come up and see what we've got," he said.

Thomas looked at Richard, and Richard looked at Henry, and Henry looked at Thomas. Then they scrambled up into the chair.

There, in a nice new nest, lay Dolly, once Mrs. Brown, then Mrs. Black, then Mrs. Gray, and now Mrs. Coaldust, and beside her were five fat, pink, naked newborn babies.

"Wow!" cried Thomas and Richard and Henry. "A ready-made noseball team!"

"You trins!" said Dolly fondly. "You really are terrible!"

ABOUT THE AUTHOR

Dick King-Smith was born and raised in Gloucestershire, England. He served in the Grenadier Guards during World War II, then returned home to Gloucestershire, to realize his lifelong ambition of farming. After twenty years as a farmer, he turned to teaching and then to writing the children's books that have earned him many fans on both sides of the Atlantic. Inspiration for his writing comes from his farm and his animals.

Among his well-loved novels are *Babe: The Gallant Pig*, *Harry's Mad*, *Martin's Mice* (each an American Library Association Notable Book); *Ace: The Very Important Pig* (a *School Library Journal* Best Book of the year); *The Toby Man*, *Paddy's Pot of Gold*, *Pretty Polly*, and *The Invisible Dog*. Additional honors and awards he has received are a *Boston Globe–Horn Book* Award (for *Babe: The Gallant Pig*) and the California Young Reader Medal (for *Harry's Mad*). In 1992, he was named Children's Author of the Year at the British Book Awards.